MW00977734

A Night

at the Inn

KERRY EVELYN

Swan Press

Copyright © 2018 by Kerry Evelyn

A Night at the Inn

Kerry Evelyn© 2018
www.KerryEvelyn.com
Kerry@KerryEvelyn.com

Published 2018 by Swan Press

Edited by Racquel Henry and Tonya Spitler
Cover by Valerie Willis, Battle Goddess Productions

All rights reserved.

Paperback ISBN: 978-0-9995861-6-7
Kindle ISBN: 978-0-9995861-7-4

*This story is dedicated to my mother, Judy,
and to my great aunt Judy Marshall Borden,
both of Fall River, Massachusetts...*

> *Lizzie Borden took an axe,*
> *Gave her mother forty whacks.*
> *When she saw what she had done,*
> *She gave her father forty-one.*

Jump Rope Chant, circa 1893, Fall River, Massachusetts

I don't believe in ghosts. But I'd do anything for Emma.

"Hey, Will! Up here!" Emma called down the steps to me.

So there we were in Fall River, Massachusetts, spending our last weekend together before I headed to Virginia for FBI training. I had big plans for the weekend, and told Emma she could choose the destination—even if it was the Lizzie Borden Bed & Breakfast.

I didn't understand her fascination for the paranormal, but if this was what it would take to advance our relationship, I was on board...literally, on board...one hundred percent.

I followed Emma up the cramped metal stairway of the battleship, across the deck, and to the railing. Her

1

wavy auburn hair whipped around her head as she turned to me. Silky tendrils licked my face like flames teasing a log in the fire, mocking the desire I'd felt for her since we met.

She grinned. Her cupid's bow smile filled me with an inner glow, her cornflower blue eyes captured mine as if pulled by magnetic forces. I knew the moment I met her I'd never look at anyone else.

"What an incredible place!" she said. "I can't believe I've lived here all my life and never explored these ships." She shuddered. "I can FEEL the essence of the sailors. Incredible."

Battleship Cove, nestled under the Braga Bridge in the historic coastal city of Fall River, was the final resting place of the USS Massachusetts and several other World War II era warships. It was eerily impressive and I found myself overcome with patriotic pride as I took in the enormity of all its former crew might have experienced. I could almost feel the spirit of the fight, the hopes and dreams of sailors long gone.

If I was one to believe in that sort of thing.

I reached for her and cupped her cheek in my hand. I pressed my forehead to hers. "Only the beginning of what I have planned for us this weekend." My lips met hers, the soft kiss a promise of more, later. "Happy birthday," I whispered.

She brought her hands up and pulled my head to hers. I lost myself in her fervent kiss as time stood still. If it wasn't our souls connecting, what else could it be? I'd never experienced a feeling so deep and consuming. My thoughts went to the velvet pouch in my pocket, and I pulled away from the kiss.

"Emma," I cradled her head in my palm and gazed into her eyes. "Six months ago, I went on a cruise with my friends, never expecting anything but a break from the Maine weather. When you tripped and spilled your wine on me, I was overcome with a feeling that I couldn't explain. It was like our souls connected, and I knew I had to get to know you better."

"I felt the same," Emma said, running her fingers through my hair. I turned my head into her hand and kissed it.

"I'm leaving Monday, and I want you to know how much I'm going to miss you and our weekends together." Just about every weekend since the cruise, Emma or I had made the trek between Crane's Cove, Maine, my hometown, to Westport, Massachusetts where she lived. We had to be together.

"I love you, Will."

"I love you, too, Emma." I slid my hand into my pocket. "So much so that I—"

A loud clang startled us apart. I whipped my head toward the sound.

"Oh! I'm so sorry! We didn't mean to interrupt," apologized the source of the noise. "Just lost my footing! I'm Marge. This is Harry," she nodded to the gentleman who had given her hand up. "Guess I don't have my sea legs yet!" Harry's lips twitched and amusement flickered in his eyes.

The couple, whom I assessed to be in their sixties, stared at us, blinking, awaiting our response.

4

"It's no problem at all. I'm Emma. This is Will." She grinned at me again and turned back to Marge. "It's great to meet you."

"Oh, likewise." Marge beamed as her eyes scanned the ships surrounding us. "Been driving over that bridge for years without stopping. It's quite an experience."

"Same here! It wasn't until this guy's curiosity got the best of him," she wrapped her arm around my waist, and I squeezed her back. "He's not from around here."

"Oh, how fun!" Marge glanced at Harry, who hadn't spoken a word, but watched his wife with adoration. I knew the feeling. "We lived up here our whole lives until we retired to Florida a few years ago. We drive up north every May for a month on the coast, then head over to visit our grandchildren on the Cape. It's been a long time since we've been here, huh, Harry?"

Harry pressed his lips, as if stifling a laugh. "That's right." He scratched behind is ear. "I don't think we've been here since the kids were little. Might think about bringing the grands here sometime. Have you been on the carousel?" His eyes twinkled as he stole a glance with his wife. She winked back at him. "Used to be a ride at Lincoln Park in the good old days. Fun place for crazy kids like us to hang out. Glad they moved it here. It's a memory-maker. Gold rings and everything."

"We'll check it out," I said. "Where's Lincoln Park?"

"Oh, it's gone now, son. Closed in the eighties. Most every ride was sold off. For a long time, all that remained was the frame of the roller coaster tracks among the overgrown land."

"I remember that!" Emma said. "I'd forgotten how spooky that thing looked from the road." She looked up at me. "Maybe sometime we could take a drive over there. I wonder if it's haunted."

Marge chuckled. "Now don't let your imagination carry you away. If you want ghosts, stay a night at Lizzie Borden's. That's where we're headed next."

Emma clasped her hands together like an excited child. "What a coincidence! We're staying there tonight, too! I've always wondered what really happened."

"Well, how 'bout that that?" Marge leaned in. "You know, I don't believe in coincidences." She tucked her arm through Harry's. "We're going to finish up our walk down Memory Lane. We'll see you two this evening."

After Marge and Harry killed the mood, I let Emma lead me around Heritage Park since I was in search of another place for my purpose. However, she hadn't slowed for a minute and I abandoned my plan for a proposal in the park.

My stomach had felt unsettled since we'd entered the Lizzie Borden Bed & Breakfast after lunch. I shook it off as nerves at first, and when it didn't subside, I questioned my choice of the local chowder.

The tour group gathered around the dining room table. We hung on to the guide's every word. "On the morning of August 4, 1892, Mr. and Mrs. Borden had their final meal at this table. They were joined by John Morse, who had arrived on Wednesday afternoon. Uncle John was the brother of Sarah Borden, Andrew Borden's first wife.

"He and Andrew had remained friendly since Sarah's death. He was from Hastings, Iowa, and he had arrived a few weeks prior and had been staying with a friend in the nearby town of Swansea. Wednesday afternoon, he came to call on the family and Abby Borden invited him to stay the night. Lizzie's stepmother set him up in the guest room, the very same room where her body was found the next day."

A chill tricked down my spine. I'd felt uneasy since we'd walked in the door. I couldn't explain it. Must be my imagination working overtime.

"Meow."

The tour guide grinned and gestured to a black cat prancing into the dining room.

"Meet Max, official cat of the Lizzie Borden Bed & Breakfast." She reached down to rub him under the chin. "Lizzie loved animals, and willed most of her money to the city for their care. She had a beloved black cat named Blackie."

The cat weaved through my legs. I bent down to scratch behind his ears and noticed his collar had a tiny sliver hatchet charm hanging from it. Max's eyes burned into mine. It was unsettling. I stood up and tuned back in to the tour.

"Lizzie did not join the family for breakfast. She was no longer taking meals with the them. No one really knows why. Some have suggested an incestuous relationship with her father. He would never let her marry. He insisted no one was good enough. There was never any evidence of this, however. Lizzie's sister was away in Fairhaven, visiting the Brownell family. She'd been out of town for the last two weeks. She spent a lot of time away."

Well, that was definitely a motive for murder.

The tour guide continued, "For a couple days leading up to the murders, the whole family had been violently ill. Mrs. Borden suspected the family might be being poisoned. Dr. Seabury Bowen lived across the street and he calmed her; told her it was probably just the food going spoiled from the heat. Breakfast that morning was mutton-broth that was several days old. It had been heated, put back in the ice chest, and reheated again and again that week. With that, they also had sugar cookies and fresh fruit, bananas and pears, johnnycakes, and coffee."

Several-days-old mutton broth? My stomach roiled. The family had money. Was Lizzie's father that much of a miser?

"What's a johnnycake?" I whispered to Emma.

The tour guide heard me. "It's a small cornmeal pancake and they are, ah, pretty indestructible. Are you not from around here?"

"No ma'am."

She nodded. "Well, you'll have to let us know tomorrow at breakfast what you think."

"Sure will."

She continued. "Mr. Morse was the first to leave

the house that morning to attend to business. Mr. Borden left shortly after. After she found her father's body on the sofa, Lizzie later told Dr. Bowen that Mrs. Borden received a note to go visit a sick friend. So no one looked for her right away. When Mrs. Borden's body was found, they brought her down here to the dining room. They laid out a sheet on top of the dining room table and placed her body on top of it.

"Mr. Borden was laid out on an undertaker's board in the sitting room where he was found, much like this one here behind me." Her hand stroked the tall, flat, narrow board that leaned against the wall behind her.

"Dr. Bowen was the first doctor on the scene. When the exams were completed, both bodies were laid side-by-side on the dining room table and covered with a sheet to await the caskets. The double funeral was held Saturday morning in the sitting room. The sofa where Mr. Borden was found had been removed from the house as evidence. The caskets were open. The undertaker had done such a good job and placed Mr. Borden's head in such a position they were able to have an open casket funeral. I can't imagine what he might have looked like. His nose had been clean sliced of and one eye had been split in half by the hatchet."

Ugh.

"Only close friends and relatives were allowed into the house for the funeral. The family sat in the front parlor greeting the guests. When the caskets left, the family filed outside. The streets were lined with people, over two thousand people followed them to Oak Grove Cemetery. Lizzie and her sister did not get out of the carriage. Only Uncle John stood by the graves. While the family was out, the police came in and did another search of the house. That's when they found the handle-less hatchet in the basement and took it into evidence."

The tour guide passed around crime scene photos of Mrs. Borden's head, Mr. Borden's body in the sitting room, and other chilling images.

"The bodies weren't buried right away. After the funeral they were taken to a receiving vault. A few days later, they were examined again by order of the mayor.

At this time, the heads were removed from the bodies. The heads were sent up to Harvard Medical School where they were examined by Dr. Dolan, the medical examiner and his assistant. They reported their findings to Hosea Knowlton, the prosecutor. Legend has it Dr. Dolan took the heads home with him where he boiled them in his basement."

It was a good thing we hadn't had dinner yet. Boiling heads?

"Take a look inside this dining room cabinet. Here we have the autopsy photos. Mr. Borden is on the left. Mrs. Borden is on the right. Contrary to the nursery rhyme, the murder weapon wasn't likely an ax, but a hatchet. Also contrary, Mr. Borden received 11 blows directly to his face. Mrs. Borden received 19. They found gold flecks in her wounds, which was odd.

"Circle around the table so that you can see the pictures and I will wait for you in the sitting room."

The sitting room proved equally chilling. This hour-long tour was taking forever. I watched Emma as the tour guide described Andrew Borden's death scene.

13

She was entranced.

"I'm going to go upstairs now. Wait till I get up there and then follow me slowly. When your eyes become level with the landing of the second floor, look to your left. Lizzie probably saw her stepmother's body before she was actually discovered. Very suspicious."

We followed her up. The door to the guest room was open, and you could see under the bed to the other side. Max's eyes glowed from where he rested, curled up under the bed.

"Many people have reported waking to the sounds of meows. And not just from Max," she added ominously.

"I've heard them," the guy with the New Bedford Paranormal logo piped up. He leaned against the door jamb. "Last time I stayed here, I could feel it, too."

"Oh dear!" Marge peered at him through her glasses. "Do you believe this house is haunted?"

"I know it for a fact," he stated. "I can prove it to you tonight if you want to join me in the basement. My team and I got high readings there last time."

"Oh!" Emma squealed. "Can we join you, too?"

"Of course. Meet me down there at nine o'clock."

The rest of the tour held the same tone. I couldn't shake the unsettling feeling. At its conclusion, we adjourned in the kitchen and were told our rooms would be ready at seven o'clock.

After dinner at Pub 99, Emma and I returned to the inn. I carried our luggage up to the third floor. At the time of the murders, only the maid's room was finished on that level. We were assigned to the Hosea Knowlton room, a pleasant enough space under the slanted roof. A portrait of the former district attorney who tried Lizzie hung to the right of a lone small window. A blue and white sunburst quilt adorned the bed, mismatched with an extra blanket adorned with printed roses. I set our suitcases on the floor next to a bin of old-fashioned toys and turned to Emma.

She was hunched over an old lamp on the bedside table. It looked to be an old oil lamp, but clicked on with the turn of a switch. "Room looks pretty authentic," I commented.

"It does fit in with the times. Did you know Mr. Borden was so cheap there were no gas or electric lights, even though they could afford it?" She straightened and tossed a smile at me over her shoulder.

"Really?"

"Yep. They had a maid, but he didn't trust her. She was an Irish immigrant. What's interesting is that they called her Maggie. They never bothered to learn her name. The maid prior to her had been named Maggie. For the three years of her employment, they called her Maggie."

"That's so mean. Why?"

"Mr. Borden was a miserable man, hated by many, and thought the Irish were beneath him. He set the tone for the women of the house. They dared not defy him."

"What a jerk."

16

"Yeah, he sounds like it." She sighed deeply and smiled at me like I was her hero. I wanted to be. "Thank you for this."

I walked up behind her and wrapped my arms around her waist. She covered my hands with hers. "Anything for you. I hope it's all you've imagined it to be," I whispered into her ears.

She shivered, and leaned back into me. "I'm sure it won't be. My imagination would scare me to death if my thoughts ever materialized!"

"Maybe it will be more than you imagined." I reached into my pocket. *Deep breath, Will.* My fingers closed around the velvet bag. "Emma, I—"

"Ahem. Er, sorry to interrupt…" Marge poked her head in. "Looks like we're floormates! And the paranormal guy is in the maid's room. Party on the third floor, woo-hoo!!"

Emma laughed. I exhaled and stepped back from her. Next time, I'd remember to shut and lock the door. "What are your plans tonight, Marge?" I asked.

"Well, Harry and I made friends with family

staying in Lizzie's suite. We're joining them for cards in the dining room in just a bit. You should come,"

"I want to explore a little," Emma said. "Catch you at nine in the basement?"

"Oh, definitely!" she said. "See ya later, alligators!"

It took Emma almost the full two hours to read, study, and examine everything that caught her interest. I watched her with fascination. She was meticulous and thorough. I was on edge. The pouch was burning a figurative hole in my pocket. I needed a Plan C. There was a winery a few miles away, and Horseneck Beach. Yes, I'd suggest a wine tasting or walk on the beach when we left the inn tomorrow.

At nine o'clock, we descended the narrow stairs to the cellar. The musty air was thick and earthy. Shawn, the paranormal guy, held a device near the display of laundry tools. The washboard leaned up against a brick wall, part of which gaped open to reveal a large basin. The bricks at the bottom crumbled outward. It was a handyman's nightmare. I wondered if it had been like this since the 1800's or staged recently when the inn opened to add to its creepy factor.

It got cold all of a sudden, and I swore for a second I could see my breath. It was only June, but it felt like the dead of winter in that basement. Emma must have felt it, too. She shook against me, eyes drawn to the device.

"Well, looks like the spirits are active tonight," Shawn said. "Take a look at the reading on my rem pod." We peered at his instrument. Several of its lights were blinking rapidly.

I felt the cat between my legs and stooped to pet it. Max's eyes glowed, reflecting off the dim overhead light. It almost felt like he was trying to tell me something. I shook my head to clear it. *It's just your imagination. There's nothing amiss here, just an old ghost story.*

Harry approached the laundry basin. He rested his hands on his knees and peered in. "Huh. Don't see nothin' but some spider webs in here."

"There's something about this wall…" Shawn

19

frowned at the reading on his device. "I'm sure of it. But what?"

"I don't know, but it sure is exciting!" Marge exclaimed. "I can't believe the rest of the folks staying here tonight passed up this chance to hunt ghosts with us. This is such a thrill!"

"It is very cool," Emma agreed. She squeezed my hand. "Let's head back up. Did you notice the toys in the corner? I've heard there's a lot of paranormal activity in there and its sometimes visited by a child ghost who drowned in the well next door."

"That's all true," Shawn interrupted. "I've never been disappointed staying in that room." What did *that* mean? "Then, let's go, Will. I don't want to miss a minute!"

I followed Emma upstairs. We changed into pajamas and settled in under the quilts. She snuggled up to me and rested her head on my chest. I kissed the top of her head. "Happy?" I asked.

"Very. Now shush." I smiled at her hopefulness.

While I agreed this place was creepy, I still didn't believe in ghosts.

Hours later, a faint meowing pulled me from a dream. I couldn't remember it, but as I opened my eyes, I felt frustrated, like I had unfinished business.

Next to my feet, the blankets suddenly depressed. "Max?" I rubbed my eyes. Odd. I didn't see the cat. And the door was closed. Had he snuck in here earlier?

"Meow."

Now it sounded as if the meowing was coming from out in the hall. My mind must be playing tricks on me.

I slid out of bed and opened the door. The door to the maid's room opened. "Did you hear that, too?" Shawn asked.

"Hear what?"

"The cat."

Okay, so it wasn't just me. "Yeah. Not sure where it went though. I felt it jump on the bed, but then I heard the sound out here. And our door has been closed. Is there another cat in the house?"

A Night at the Inn

"Not any living ones."

Shawn and I jerked our heads in the direction of the stairwell at the sound of another meow. "That has to be Max yowling."

The third door opened. Harry poked his head out. "What's the ruckus? Can't get any sleep around here," he grumbled.

"Will?" Emma called. "What's going on?"

"It's the cat," I said. The yowling was definitely coming from the second floor stairwell. Odd that none of the guests on the second floor had awakened. Or they just didn't care.

Emma climbed out of bed. "I didn't hear the cat. But maybe Max is supposed to go out at night? To hunt? We should let him out."

"All right. Let me grab my shoes."

Shawn led the way down the back stairs of the old house. Emma and I were right behind him, followed by Harry and the addition of Marge, who had slipped out to join her husband. The sound led us to the sitting room on the first floor, where it abruptly stopped.

"Max?" Emma called. "Here, kitty, kitty…" She looked up. "I still don't hear him."

"This way," Shawn led the group to the kitchen. The last time this happened, the meowing led me down to the cellar."

"This has happened before?" I asked

"Yeah. And I never see Max. It's like he's a ghost."

Emma crossed her arms and shivered. "Creepy."

"There's no such thing as ghosts," I stated firmly.

"How do you know?" she asked.

I didn't answer.

Sure enough, the next meow seemed to be coming from below. The door to the cellar was ajar. For the second time that night, the four of us followed Shawn down the stairs. Over by the laundry basin, I heard it again.

"Look at the back wall," Shawn pointed. "Do you see the face?"

We all leaned in. You could barely make out the outline of a face in back wall of the white brick

23

structure.

Something rustled. "Do you hear that?" I asked. They all looked at me blankly. "The scratching sound?" They shook their heads. How could they not hear it? I crouched down and peered into the space. It sounded like it was coming from under the laundry bin.

I placed my hands on the rim of the bin and lifted. "Ow." It wouldn't budge.

"What are you doing?" Emma hissed. "You're not supposed to touch that."

Shawn gripped it and attempted to dislodge it. "It's cemented in."

"Why would they do that?" Marge asked. "If I had to do laundry in that thing, I'd want to move it out."

"There's something under it," I insisted. "I can hear it." I grabbed hold of a crumbling whitewashed brick. It was loose.

"Well, let's try to move it then," Harry suggested.

Shawn pulled the laundry paddle off the hook on the wall and used it as a makeshift lever. We worked together to dislodge the basin.

"Look!" I brushed the dust away.

"I knew it!" Shawn was gleeful. "Let me help."

Together, we lifted out a metal box and set it down on top of a nearby table. Harry found a flathead screwdriver on a dusty shelf that held modern tools. "Let me pry that open for you."

"Wait," Emma said. "We should probably call someone, don't you think?"

"No way." Shawn was firm. "We can put it back when we're done and then call. I've been waiting for years for something like this. If we call someone, we'll never see what's inside."

"Be what about fingerprints? And what if they don't believe us because we've compromised the scene?"

"I'm not worried, Emma," Shawn assured her. "Just be careful, Harry. Don't damage it."

Harry humphed. "Don't you worry, young lady." We watched as he loosed the lid. "All set. Pull it off."

Shawn lifted the lid off. Inside, the skeleton of a cat

laid atop a folded sheet of paper, yellowed with age. "Holy…"

"Wow," Emma whispered. Marge and Harry looked on with equal wonderment.

Carefully, so as to not disrupt the bones, Shawn slid out the paper. He unfolded it. "*Confession of Lizzie Andrew Borden.* No way…"

"Well, read it!" Marge insisted.

Shawn held up to the dim light above. His eyes scanned the flowery script. "I'm not reading this out loud. You all can read it yourselves."

He handed it to me when he was done. No way was I reading it. I didn't even want to touch it. Emma read over my shoulder. "I'll read it," she said to Harry and Marge.

"*Confession of Lizzie Andrew Borden. Here lies the remains of my most beloved pet. He belongs here; I just can't bear to bring him to Maplecroft. May his memory live forever.*"

"And his meows," I said.

"Shh, Will!" Emma continued, *"Now that I've been acquitted, I feel the need to get the real story off my chest. I pray this is not discovered in my lifetime, or during the lifetime of my beloved Seabury.* No way! Her *beloved* Seabury? He was twenty years older than her and married!"

"Go on, Emma," I urged her.

"We had laid the best plans. After the poisoning didn't work, we decided we'd have to kill them with force. My sister wanted no part of it, so she decided to stay with the Brownells. It was Excursion Day for the Fall River Police Department, and they would be understaffed by half. Uncle John had stayed over, and I knew that would delay my stepmother's plans for the day, as she couldn't go about her errands until the guest room had been made up. I wasn't worried about Maggie coming in; Father insisted the women of the family clean and care for the second level. Maggie did not have access to our rooms and was not allowed on the second floor.

"Father would come home, as he'd been doing

lately, and doze on the couch before lunch. Seabury had sent his driver to drive to Tiverton and back, and paid him well to never give away that the good doctor was not in his carriage.

"While Maggie was outside, Seabury struck my stepmother down, but she kept moving, even after several hatchet strikes to her face. I watched from the doorway, fascinated at how numb and detached I felt. She'd gotten what she deserved. When he finished, I hustled him down the back stairs to the cellar, where we waited for father to come home. Maggie had finished washing the windows by then, and she told Father that Mrs. Borden (I shall never and have never referred to her as Mother) had received a note to visit a sick friend. Still feeling ill, no doubt from the poison and washing the windows in the heat, she then went up the back steps to her room to lie down. She never even suspected."

"Wow," Marge breathed. "So cold."

I felt it, too. The basement's temperature had dropped from cool to frigid.

"My father's life left him very quickly. At the start of his snores, Seabury was upon him, and then back in the basement. We set to work cleaning ourselves up, and then I went to the barn to establish my alibi. I wrapped the blade in my dress, and Seabury placed it in the bottom of his medical bag, never to be seen again. The one that was found was old, and was never proven to be the murder weapon. We'd gotten shiny new one for the occasion, complete with gold foil along the edge of the blade."

"Incredible," Harry said. "After all this time…"

I squeezed Emma's hand. "I didn't understand why this was so important to you. I get it now. You can't help but want to know what really happened." She pressed her lips together and squeezed my hand back.

"Father had disapproved of Seabury all those years ago. Too old for me, he said. But we were soulmates and kindred spirits. We still are.

I felt bad for Lizzie. Emma was my soulmate. I couldn't imagine how I'd feel if I had to go through life without her by my side. Dr. Bowen and his family lived

29

across the street. So close, yet unreachable and off-limits. Her heart must have shattered daily. I thought about the ring in my pocket and glanced around the damp cellar. I swallowed hard, and considered the timing—it wasn't right. Not tonight. Maybe not tomorrow, either.

Suddenly, the hairs on my neck pricked. I shivered. My head swelled as a warm sensation filled it. I glanced up. I didn't want to believe. I'd spent my whole life avoiding graveyards and funerals. Two iridescent eyes glowed back at me from the tool shelf.

"You knew. You always knew," I said.

"Will, who are you talking to?" Emma asked.

"Up there. The cat."

"I don't see a cat."

Lizzie Borden, circa 1893

92 Second St., 1893 and present day

A Night at the Inn

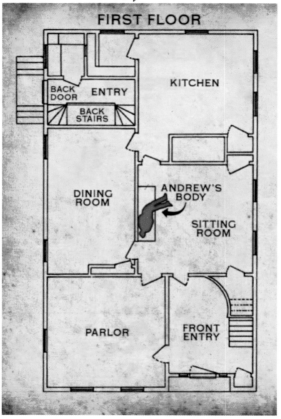

FIRST FLOOR

BACK DOOR

ENTRY

BACK STAIRS

KITCHEN

DINING ROOM

ANDREW'S BODY

SITTING ROOM

PARLOR

FRONT ENTRY

Illustration by Ray Keim, adapted from E. Porter,
Fall River Tragedy (1893)

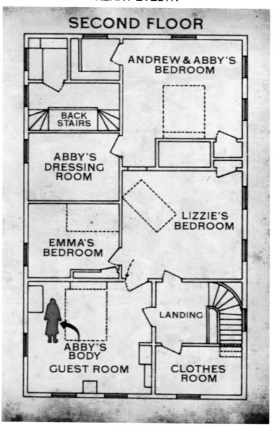

SECOND FLOOR

ANDREW & ABBY'S BEDROOM

BACK STAIRS

ABBY'S DRESSING ROOM

LIZZIE'S BEDROOM

EMMA'S BEDROOM

LANDING

ABBY'S BODY

GUEST ROOM

CLOTHES ROOM

Andrew Borden   *Abby Borden*

Hatchet found at the Borden Residence, 1892

KERRY EVELYN

Parlor, August 4, 1892

Guest Room, August 4, 1892

A Night at the Inn

Parlor, Present Day   Photo by Debbie Drolet

Guest Room, Present Day   Photo by Debbie Drolet

Lizzie Borden   *Dr. Seabury Bowen*

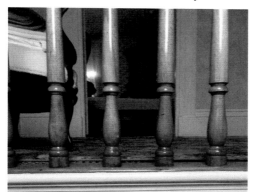

View of the Guest Room from the Stairs
Photo by Debbie Drolet

A Night at the Inn

This picture inspired the story. Do you see the face?
Photo by Debbie Drolet

Acknowledgements

Thanks to L.E. Perez for giving me the opportunity to write this story for *Thrill of the Hunt 4: Urban Legends Re-Imagined.* It was fun to stretch my creativity and suggest an alternate theory to the folks at home! I'm very grateful to my friends and my team who helped me bring this story to life.

To Racquel Henry, Tonya Spitler, and Chelsea Fuchs, thank you for your never-ending support, encouragement, and advice on everything I write, especially at weird hours of the day and night when ideas or panic strike. It's nice to know I'm not the only one with sleeping issues, haha!

Mom and Laura, brainstorming with you is so fun, and I'm so glad for the help fleshing this story out. It's so cool to have familial ties to a creepy story!

A Night at the Inn

I could not have written this tale without the help of two of my local friends. Debbie Drolet, I'm infinitely grateful to you for sharing your "inside" info, photos, and knowledge. Huge thanks to my favorite "paranormal guy," my old friend Shawn Sullivan of New Bedford Paranormal, who gave me a glimpse of the "other side" and fueled my imagination.

Thanks to Val, who helped me fix the mess I created when I attempted to put this altogether myself. I vow to here on out leave the techy artistic stuff to the most talented, patient, and kind graphic designer I know! XOXO! *(Valerie here: It's ok! I love you too!)*

And finally, to my narrator, Jennifer Swanepoel, for taking a chance on a new author and bringing my characters to life. This is just the beginning!

About the Author

Kerry Evelyn has always been fascinated by people and the backstories that drive them to do what they do. A native of the Massachusetts SouthCoast, she changed her latitude in 2002 and is now a crazy blessed wife and homeschooling mom in Orlando. She loves God, books of all kinds, traveling, taking selfies, sweet drinks, and escaping into her imagination, where every child is happy and healthy, every house has a library, and her hubby wears coattails and a top hat 24/7.

KerryEvelyn.com
Facebook.com/KerryEvelynAuthor
Instagram: @KerryEvelynAuthor
Twitter: @TheKerryEvelyn

Made in the USA
Columbia, SC
12 August 2022

65212926R00027